Pick a Powerpuff Path

# bubbles in the middle

by Aaron Rosenberg

Scholastic Inc.
New York • Toronto • London • Auckland • Sydney
Mexico City • New Delhi • Hong Kong • Buenos Aires

ISBN 0-439-33261-3

Copyright © 2002 by Cartoon Network.

CARTOON NETWORK, the logo, THE POWERPUFF GIRLS, and all related characters and elements are trademarks of and © Cartoon Network.

(s02)

Published by Scholastic Inc. All rights reserved.

SCHOLASTIC and associated logos are trademarks and/or registered trademarks of Scholastic Inc.

Cover and interior illustrations by Christopher Cook

Inked by Michele Parrish-McKnight

Designed by Mark Neston

12 11 10 9 8 7 6 5 4 3 2 1          2 3 4 5 6 7/0

Printed in the U. S. A.

First Scholastic printing, August 2002

# Read This First!

*Sugar...Spice...and Everything Nice...*

*These were the ingredients chosen to create the perfect little girl. But Professor Utonium accidentally added an extra ingredient to the concoction—Chemical X!*

*And thus, The Powerpuff Girls were born! Using their ultra superpowers, Blossom, Bubbles, and Buttercup have dedicated their lives to fighting crime and the forces of evil!*

*But now, The Powerpuff Girls need your help! In every Pick a Powerpuff Path, you will take on the role of one of the characters and help save the day.*

*In this adventure, you will be Bubbles, the sweetest of The Powerpuff Girls. But Bubbles has a problem: Blossom and Buttercup can't stop arguing with each other! And that means they're not doing a good job of protecting Townsville. It's up to Bubbles to get her sisters to work together. But will Blossom and Buttercup stop quarreling long enough to listen to her?*

*It's up to you to determine what happens throughout Bubbles's day and how well Buttercup and Blossom get along. The story will be different depending on the choices you make. When one adventure ends, you can start over and make new choices to read a completely different story. Time to get started turning pages—there's no argument about that!*

It was another beautiful morning, and the city was waking up. In their bedroom, The Powerpuff Girls were waking up as well. Bubbles was cheerful, as usual. But Buttercup and Blossom had stayed up late last night—Buttercup to watch a monster movie and Blossom to finish the science book she was reading—and the lack of sleep had left both of them grumpy.

"I get to brush my teeth first," Buttercup insisted, pushing past her sisters on the way to the bathroom.

"No, I do," said Blossom, pushing right back.

"I've already brushed my teeth," Bubbles replied. "I'm going downstairs."

When Buttercup and Blossom came downstairs to breakfast, they were both still grumpy and still arguing.

"Pass the cereal," Blossom said, reaching to take the box from Bubbles.

"I'm hungrier, so I should get it first!" Buttercup argued, grabbing the box from Blossom.

"Can't you guys just take turns nicely?" Bubbles asked, eating her cereal, but her sisters weren't listening.

"Professor, can't you make them stop fighting?" Bubbles wailed.

"What's that, Bubbles?" Professor Utonium asked, looking up absentmindedly. The Professor was trying to shove two large stacks of papers into his briefcase at the same time, and papers were flying everywhere.

"Now, remember, Girls, I'm speaking at the Inventors' Conference today, but I should be home by the time school is over," the Professor said. "What an honor! I hope I've got all my notes. You Girls behave, and have a nice day at school."

Bubbles sighed. Clearly the Professor wasn't going to be any help in getting her sisters to stop quarreling! The three Girls kissed the Professor good-bye, and then zoomed off to school. As they flew, Buttercup kept turning around in the air to glare at Blossom.

The Girls spent the morning working on their reading and math. Then their teacher, Ms. Keane, announced that it was arts and crafts time—Bubbles's favorite subject! But Bubbles didn't enjoy arts and crafts today, because trouble started soon after everyone got out their crayons, markers, paints, and glue. Buttercup and Blossom both wanted to use the blue crayon, and they grabbed for it at the same time.

"Give it to me!" Buttercup insisted.

"I had it first!" Blossom claimed. The two Girls tugged the small crayon back and forth.

"Girls, there's no need to fight over the same crayon!" Ms. Keane told them. "There are other crayons." But Blossom and Buttercup didn't answer her, or even seem to hear her. "Bubbles, can you please talk to your sisters? You're probably the only one they'll listen to right now."

"I'll try," Bubbles promised. *But will they really listen to me when they're this mad?* she wondered. *Maybe I should just take the crayon from them, so that neither of them has it to fight over.*

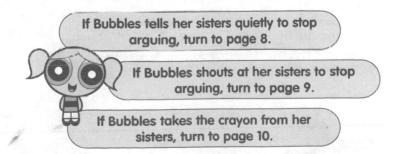

If Bubbles tells her sisters quietly to stop arguing, turn to page 8.

If Bubbles shouts at her sisters to stop arguing, turn to page 9.

If Bubbles takes the crayon from her sisters, turn to page 10.

"Can you guys *please* stop fighting?" Bubbles pleaded with her sisters, but her voice was so soft and gentle that they didn't even seem to hear her. Instead, they kept arguing and tugging at the crayon.

"I'm sorry, Ms. Keane," Bubbles said to their teacher. "Blossom and Buttercup won't listen to me, either."

"That's all right, Bubbles—you tried your best," said Ms. Keane kindly. "Maybe if we just leave them alone, they'll stop."

Bubbles sighed, nodded, and went back to coloring. It was a good thing *she* didn't need the color blue for her picture! Then, out of the corner of her eye, she noticed something moving outside the window, out past the playground. As Bubbles floated toward the window, she saw what looked like a giant dog outside! Bubbles thought that the Girls should probably find out what it was. Would Blossom and Buttercup stop arguing if she told them about the dog? Bubbles just wasn't sure.

If Bubbles decides to investigate the dog by herself, turn to page 27.

If Bubbles decides to ask her sisters to help her investigate the dog, turn to page 28.

8

Talking to her sisters quietly wouldn't work, Bubbles decided—Blossom and Buttercup were too busy arguing to hear her. So she took a deep breath and shouted, "Knock it off!"

For a moment, both Buttercup and Blossom stopped what they were doing. Bubbles *never* shouted! They stared at her, surprised. But then Buttercup, leaning back to look at Bubbles, pulled the blue crayon with her. Blossom's grip tightened in response, and the two went back to fighting. Then The Powerpuff Girls' hotline phone rang.

"Got it!" Blossom announced, releasing the crayon and flying to the phone. Buttercup clutched the crayon and stuck out her tongue, but Blossom ignored her.

"Hello, Mayor?" said Blossom into the phone. "What's that? Okay, we're on it."

Blossom hung up the phone and turned to her sisters. "That was the Mayor. The Gangreen Gang's causing trouble at the park. Let's go."

Buttercup took a last look at the blue crayon, and tossed it on the table. "Fine. But that crayon's *mine* when we get back."

Then the three Girls flew out of the room, toward the park.

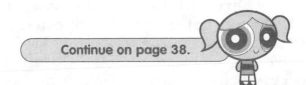

Continue on page 38.

Bubbles wished that Ms. Keane was right, that her sisters *would* listen to her. But when Blossom and Buttercup were quarreling, they wouldn't listen to *anyone*. So instead, Bubbles reached out and grabbed the blue crayon from them.

*"Hey!"* they both shouted, surprised—Bubbles was the last person *anyone* would expect to grab anything from other people.

"Give that back!" Buttercup demanded.

"Yeah, give it here!" Blossom agreed.

Just then the door to the classroom opened, and a man walked in. He was middle-aged, with dark hair and a mustache. Bubbles recognized him as the head baker from Townsville Bakery. But what was he doing here at school?

"Give me all your money," the baker demanded. "I need to give it to Mojo."

Bubbles gasped in surprise. Why was the baker asking for money to give to Mojo Jojo, the monkey supervillain?

"I'm sorry, we don't have any money," Ms. Keane replied. "This is a classroom, not a bank."

"Oh." The baker turned around and walked away without another word.

*How strange*, thought Bubbles.

"We'd better follow him," Blossom said, and for the first time that morning Buttercup agreed with her. Ms. Keane gave The Powerpuff Girls permission to leave the classroom, and the three Girls flew outside, keeping the baker in sight.

The Girls watched as the baker walked into a jewelry store. "Give me all of your money," the baker told the salespeople. "I need to give it to my best friend, Mojo Jojo, the greatest of all monkey super-geniuses."

"Okay, that's it," Buttercup said, zooming into the store and gripping the baker's collar. "I don't care if you *do* make good cookies, I'm *not* letting you rob a jewelry store!" The baker didn't even resist. He just stared blankly at the Girls.

"Now, what's this all about?" Blossom said sternly.

"I need to give my best friend, Mojo Jojo, all the money I can get," the baker repeated.

"Do you owe him money for something?" wondered Bubbles aloud.

"No, he just asked me to get him some money," said the baker. "Mojo Jojo is the greatest of all monkey super-geniuses, you know!"

The Girls looked at one another. The baker liked Mojo and wanted to give him money? Why? Something wasn't right here. But what should they do?

If Bubbles suggests the Girls go look for Mojo, turn to page 16.

If Bubbles decides to give the baker some money, hoping that it will help her figure out his strange behavior, turn to page 12.

"Let the baker go. I have an idea," Bubbles told Buttercup. Bubbles then pulled out a dollar and gave it to the baker. "Here," Bubbles said to him. "Here's some money. Go give it to Mojo Jojo."

"Thanks," the baker said, smiling.

"Why are you giving him money?" asked Buttercup. "He was *stealing!*"

"Well, I thought that we could follow the baker when he brings the money to Mojo. Then we could find Mojo and figure out what's going on," explained Bubbles to her sisters in a whisper, so the baker wouldn't overhear her.

"Good idea," Blossom agreed. "But maybe the baker will just tell us where Mojo is." She turned back to the would-be thief.

"Where's Mojo?" Blossom asked the baker. But the baker shook his head.

"I can't tell you—Mojo's my friend! I have to go give him this money!" the baker said stubbornly, and continued out the door. The Girls quietly followed the baker through the streets of Townsville. Soon they found themselves nearing the bank, and sure enough, there was evil monkey super-genius Mojo Jojo. He was standing just outside the bank, his cape swirling about him. A large radio sat on the ground next to him, playing something the Girls couldn't quite hear, and he was surrounded by a strange greenish cloud—it looked like some kind of gas. People were walking up and giving Mojo money and valuables, which he directed them to deposit in the bags behind him. He hadn't noticed the Girls yet!

"Let's just fly in and get him," Buttercup suggested.

"But what's that funny-looking cloud down there?" Blossom wondered aloud. "I think we should take care of that first."

"Maybe we can sneak up on Mojo," Bubbles said, "while he's not looking."

If Bubbles agrees with Buttercup that they should go after Mojo directly, turn to page 48.

If Bubbles agrees with Blossom that they should get rid of the cloud first, turn to page 22.

If Bubbles sticks with her plan to sneak up on Mojo, turn to page 56.

"Blossom is right," Bubbles declared. "The animals aren't our enemy—Mojo Jojo is!"

The Girls grabbed the evil monkey super-genius and snatched the device from his belt. Blossom looked it over quickly and pressed two buttons. The animals immediately stopped attacking and relaxed, and their flames went away.

"Wow!" Buttercup muttered. "I guess the device made them breathe fire, too!"

Blossom smashed the device in her hands and said, "Girls, destroy the animals' collars, too. The device was transmitting to them."

Buttercup and Bubbles quickly broke the animals' collars.

*"We're sorry,"* the animals told Bubbles. *"We didn't want to hurt anyone. It was the collars!"*

*"I know,"* Bubbles replied. *"But those are gone now."*

*"Thank you,"* the animals told her.

"Where will you go now?" asked Bubbles.

"To the woods," the dog said. "There's plenty of space there for us to roam around, and we won't bother anybody—or be bothered. We'll keep to ourselves."

"Okay. Be good." Bubbles waved good-bye, and the animals left.

"Too bad we couldn't keep them as pets," Bubbles said sadly.

"Where would we put them?" Buttercup said, giggling. "I remember when you tried to bring home a baby whale! I don't think you should bring home any pets unless they actually *fit* into the house."

Then the Girls took Mojo to jail, where he belonged!

Afterward, Buttercup turned to Blossom. "That was smart, figuring out how the device worked," she admitted.

"Well, you did a great job keeping the animals back so I could get to it," Blossom said.

"Yeah, and without Bubbles talking to the animals, we wouldn't have known what was going on," Buttercup pointed out. "I guess we really *do* work well together, don't we?"

"Well, we *are* sisters," Blossom replied. She smiled. "I'm sorry I've been behaving so badly today."

"Me, too," said Buttercup.

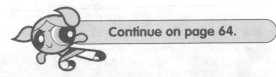

Continue on page 64.

"We've got to find Mojo!" said Bubbles.

"But what should we do about the baker?" wondered Blossom aloud.

"I guess we should put him behind bars, at least until we figure out what's going on," Buttercup suggested, and they carried the baker off to jail.

"Okay, so now what do we do?" Buttercup demanded. "We still don't know where Mojo is."

"He's probably not at his lair—Mojo knows that's the first place we'll look," Blossom replied. "We'll just have to fly around town and look for him."

"That's a snap," Buttercup called back, floating up so she looked down on her two sisters. "I'm the fastest one—*I'll* find Mojo Jojo."

"*You*, the fastest?" Blossom laughed. "I don't *think* so!"

"Am too!" Buttercup insisted.

"Are not!" Blossom replied.

"You think you can beat me? Prove it!" Buttercup shouted.

"Fine, I will!" cried Blossom.

The two Girls each took a deep breath, clearly about to start racing.

*Now* what was Bubbles going to do? Bubbles wanted to stay with her sisters, but she didn't want to race with them—finding Mojo was more important than seeing who was faster!

If Bubbles races with her sisters so that she can keep up with them, turn to page 17.

If Bubbles refuses to race, turn to page 39.

*Well, I guess we'll find Mojo faster if we fly faster,* Bubbles decided. She also hoped that if she stayed with her sisters, she might still be able to convince them to stop arguing. So she floated up to join them.

"Ready," Buttercup shouted.

"Set," Blossom replied.

"Go!" Bubbles announced, getting into the spirit of the race. And they were off!

The three of them zoomed around the city at top speed, from one end of Townsville to the other and back. People all throughout the city stopped to look up as their protectors raced past overhead.

Eventually, the Girls started to get tired and stopped for a rest on a nearby cloud. No one seemed to be the winner.

"I...guess...it's a...draw," Buttercup gasped.

"For...now," Blossom agreed.

"Did...anyone...see...Mojo?" Bubbles managed to ask, still struggling for breath.

Unfortunately, none of them had. They'd been moving so fast, they hadn't seen much of anything! But now the Girls looked down and saw a bunch of people standing around in front of the bank.

"What's going on here?" Blossom asked the crowd as the Girls flew down.

Continue on page 18.

"We like Mojo," a skinny man replied. "He is our best friend, and the greatest of all monkey super-geniuses."

"Yes, we want to give him all the money in our bank accounts," a tall woman said.

"When our bank accounts are empty, we're going to steal more money for Mojo Jojo," a stout man said, and everyone else agreed. The people at the bank were all acting like the baker—Mojo Jojo must have brainwashed all of them somehow!

"Where is Mojo now?" Blossom asked the crowd.

"He left with the money we gave him," someone said. "We like him."

"Great," Buttercup growled. "Mojo's got everyone's money, and we've missed him!"

"Well, we'd better lock everyone up for now," Blossom decided. "Otherwise, they might try stealing more money for Mojo." The Girls carted everyone off to jail. Then they flew after Mojo, and found him inside his Volcano Top Observatory, after all. Mojo was counting an enormous pile of cash and other valuables.

"This is a surprise, Girls!" Mojo called out as The Powerpuff Girls flew in. "What are you doing here? I am not causing any trouble, just counting my money, which is to say, the money that belongs to me, Mojo Jojo."

"Somehow I don't think that money—or those valuables—belong to you," Blossom replied. "I think you stole them—or brainwashed other people to steal them for you!"

As the Girls carried Mojo off to jail again, the monkey mastermind, who could never resist a good speech, bragged about his "nearly perfect plan" to use some kind of mysterious gas cloud to brainwash the citizens of Townsville into stealing for him. The Girls locked Mojo up with all of the brainwashed people. Fortunately, the effects of the gas cloud were only temporary—after a few hours, everyone was back to normal, and they were all allowed out of jail. Except for Mojo, who stayed in jail, of course! Then the Girls returned all the money and valuables to their rightful owners.

"If you hadn't been determined to race each other," Bubbles reminded her sisters, "we could have gotten to Mojo *before* he'd brainwashed everyone."

Her sisters both hung their heads.

"You're right. I was being silly, letting competition get in the way of doing our job," Blossom said.

"I'm sorry, too," Buttercup said.

Continue on page 64.

*I don't need my sisters to help me take care of Mojo,* Bubbles decided. *Besides, they'll just fight with each other the whole time and get in my way.* She flew into the cloud, determined to grab Mojo on her own. But as soon as Bubbles entered the greenish cloud, she began to feel funny. A moment later, Bubbles settled to the ground in front of a grinning Mojo.

"Hello, Bubbles. How are you today?" Mojo asked.

"I'm fine, thank you, greatest of all monkey super-geniuses," Bubbles said cheerfully. "Would you like some money, best friend Mojo?"

"Why, that is *very* thoughtful of you, Bubbles!" Mojo replied. "Yes, I *would* like—"

Then Bubbles spotted her two sisters, who were floating just outside the cloud. *Too bad,* thought Bubbles. *Wouldn't it be nice if Blossom and Buttercup flew into the pretty green cloud, too?*

"Bubbles," Blossom called out, "what are you doing with Mojo?"

"Yeah," Buttercup said. "Why don't you grab him? He's right there!"

Bubbles hadn't grabbed Mojo because she *liked* Mojo—he was her friend. But for some reason, Bubbles wasn't sure she could tell her sisters that.

If Bubbles tells her sisters that Mojo is her best friend now, turn to page 53.

If Bubbles gives her sisters a different reason why she hasn't grabbed Mojo, turn to page 54.

*I'd better wait until Blossom and Buttercup get back before I do anything,* Bubbles decided. She flew around the corner and used her X-ray vision to spy on Mojo through the bank's wall. After a few minutes, Blossom and Buttercup came down to join her.

"I won, I'm telling you," Buttercup was saying.

"You did not—I was in front," Blossom insisted.

"Never mind that," Bubbles told them. "I've found Mojo. He's at the bank. He's got some kind of green gas cloud around him. And he's got a radio, too. I think he's using the cloud and the radio to brainwash all these people."

Buttercup and Blossom looked over at Mojo, who was still busy taking people's money.

"I say we get him," Buttercup said.

"But that gas cloud looks bad," Blossom replied. "We should get rid of that first."

"Maybe we should sneak up on him," Bubbles suggested, "since he hasn't seen us yet."

'Well, *my* plan's better," Blossom insisted.

"No, *mine* is," said Buttercup.

"Fine!" Bubbles announced. "Since you two can't agree, *I'll* decide."

If Bubbles decides to go after Mojo directly, as Buttercup suggested, turn to page 48.

If Bubbles decides to go for the gas cloud, as Blossom suggested, turn to page 22.

If Bubbles decides to sneak up on Mojo, as she herself suggested, turn to page 56.

"I agree with Blossom," Bubbles decided. "We should get rid of the gas cloud first."

"Whatever," Buttercup grumbled.

"Okay, but how should we get rid of it?" Blossom wondered aloud. She thought for a second. "We could use our eye beams on it, and try to burn it off."

"We could spin around the gas cloud and create a tornado," Buttercup offered. "That'd be cool, and it'd suck up all the gas; then, we could spin it away from everyone!"

Both ideas sounded good to Bubbles. But, of course, Buttercup and Blossom refused to consider each other's idea.

If Bubbles decides they should blast the gas cloud with their eye beams, as Blossom suggested, turn to page 23.

If Bubbles decides they should spin up a tornado to suck up the gas cloud, as Buttercup suggested, turn to page 60.

22

"I think using our eye beams is a good idea," Bubbles said. "A tornado might damage the building and hurt some of the people nearby."

"You *always* side with her," Buttercup complained, but she went along with the plan. The Girls flew down toward the strange green cloud of gas. When they were floating just in front of the cloud, all three Girls focused on it, and their eyes began to glow. Beams shot from their eyes, striking the gas cloud. Wherever the Girls' eye beams touched, the gas began to burn away, leaving only clean air. But after a few minutes, Bubbles glanced around. *There's an awful lot of this gas,* she thought, *and it's taking a long time to get rid of it. Maybe we should try something different.*

If Bubbles decides they should concentrate their eye beams together on a single tiny spot of the gas cloud, turn to page 50.

If Bubbles decides they should separate and attack different areas of the gas cloud, turn to page 26.

23

"We've got to find out more about this lab experiment—who knows what other things have been done to this sweet doggie!" said Bubbles to her sisters.

"Hey, what's that?" Buttercup asked suddenly, pointing at the dog's collar, which was very strange-looking. It was metal, with oddly shaped pieces sticking out in several spots. It looked less like a collar and more like some sort of machine.

"I don't know, but whatever it is, it can't be good," Blossom replied. "Let's use our eye beams on it, Girls!" All three Girls focused their eye beams on the collar. With a small pop, the collar's buckle melted, and the collar dropped to the ground. The dog immediately started wagging its tail.

*"Thank you,"* the dog told Bubbles. *"That collar was starting to hurt, and it was sending out these weird signals—it was telling me to wreck things!"*

*"That's terrible,"* Bubbles replied. *"Who would do this to you?"*

*"I don't know his name,"* the dog said, *"but he was a monkey, and he wore a big helmet on his head."*

"Of course, it was Mojo Jojo who did this nasty thing to this poor doggie!" Bubbles said to her sisters.

"It figures!" said Buttercup, disgusted. "Only Mojo would think of something like this!"

*"May I go now?"* the dog asked. *"I promise not to cause any more trouble—I'll go off into the woods, where I won't bother anyone—or be bothered."*

*"Good-bye! Be good!"* Bubbles called after the large dog as they watched it leave.

"Nice job, Bubbles," Blossom admitted. "Trying to talk to the dog first was a smart idea."

"Yeah," Buttercup agreed. "I guess it was better than fighting the dog for no reason."

"Thanks," Bubbles told her sisters. "But we all work together. Each of us can do things the others can't—that's why we're a team."

"She's right," Blossom said.

"Yeah. I'm sorry I've been so grumpy today," said Buttercup.

"Me, too," said Blossom, hugging Buttercup.

"Great!" Bubbles said. "Now let's go get Mojo!"

The Girls found Mojo in a pet store—about to buy another dog to replace the one who had just escaped—and put him in jail.

Continue on page 64.

Bubbles motioned to her sisters. "This is just taking too long. If we separate and each go for a part of the gas cloud, maybe we can burn away the gas more quickly!"

Buttercup and Blossom nodded at that and flew to opposite sides, still using their eye beams.

"Ha! My eye beams are stronger than yours!" Buttercup taunted.

"They are not!" Blossom shouted back.

Bubbles just sighed and kept working.

Their eye beams were burning off the cloud, but there was simply too much of the green gas, and it kept creeping toward them, making them cough as it got closer. Then Bubbles heard Buttercup shout, "This isn't working—let's just get him!"

Continue on page 48.

Since Blossom and Buttercup were still fighting over the crayon, Bubbles decided to investigate the giant dog on her own. *They'll never stop arguing long enough to listen to me,* she thought.

"Excuse me, Ms. Keane, but I need to go check on something," Bubbles announced, flying out the window.

"That's fine, Bubbles—just don't be long!" Ms. Keane called after her. Blossom and Buttercup didn't even notice Bubbles was gone.

Once outside, Bubbles looked around. She zipped off in the direction where she thought she had seen the dog. Then she rounded a corner and gasped at what she saw.

"It *is* a doggie," she whispered to herself. But not just any dog. This dog, which had short brown fur, floppy ears and a big bushy tail, was the size of a truck! Maybe it was a nice dog, and if Bubbles used her ability to speak to animals to talk to it, she would find that out. But if the dog was a mean dog, Bubbles would definitely need her sisters' help!

If Bubbles decides to talk to the dog, turn to page 34.

If Bubbles decides to get her sisters' help right away, turn to page 28.

27

Bubbles returned to Blossom and Buttercup, who were still fighting over the crayon.

"Forget about the crayon," Bubbles insisted. "Townsville needs us—there's a huge dog outside our classroom!"

"What?" That made Buttercup drop the crayon. "Show me!"

"I'm coming, too!" Blossom said, and the three of them flew outside together.

"It's right over there," Bubbles whispered, pointing. Buttercup and Blossom were so impressed by the size of the dog that they hesitated to move any closer.

"Wow, it's huge!" Buttercup whispered. "I say we capture the dog before it causes any trouble. We can take it to the zoo or something."

"It doesn't seem to be hurting anyone," Blossom replied. "We should just watch it for a while and see what it's up to before we go after it."

"Maybe I can just talk to the dog," Bubbles suggested, but her sisters didn't hear her because they were too busy arguing over which of their ideas was better. *They'll never agree,* Bubbles thought. *I'll have to decide for all of us.*

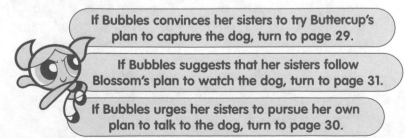

If Bubbles convinces her sisters to try Buttercup's plan to capture the dog, turn to page 29.

If Bubbles suggests that her sisters follow Blossom's plan to watch the dog, turn to page 31.

If Bubbles urges her sisters to pursue her own plan to talk to the dog, turn to page 30.

As much as she loved animals, Bubbles knew that a dog that size could be dangerous. So Bubbles said, "I think Buttercup might be right—we should stop the dog before it hurts anyone."

"Yeah!" Buttercup said, and charged toward the dog, followed by her sisters. Bubbles heard Blossom mutter something like, "I'm supposed to be the leader—why doesn't anyone want to follow *my* plan?"

As the Girls approached, the dog turned to face them. Flames shot out of its mouth, right toward the Girls! Blossom, Bubbles, and Buttercup quickly dodged out of the way. It seemed that the dog really *was* dangerous.

All three Girls swooped in again, intending to grab the dog from behind, but it turned quickly and faced them once more, breathing fire directly at them, so the Girls had to veer off again. Although the dog's flames missed the Girls, fire did strike several trees. Thick gray smoke billowed from the burning trees. By the time the Girls headed back toward the dog, the entire street was filled with smoke.

"Oh, great!" Buttercup complained as the Girls came to a stop. "Where did the dog go?"

The Girls peered around, but they couldn't see the dog at all. Had it escaped somehow?

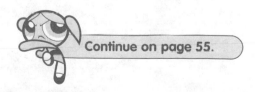

Continue on page 55.

"Let me talk to the dog first," Bubbles insisted. "Maybe it's just lost. I'm sure it doesn't mean us any harm."

"Oh, whatever," Buttercup replied.

"Sure, fine," Blossom agreed. Neither of them seemed very enthusiastic, but at least they'd agreed on something.

"*Hello,*" Bubbles said as she approached the dog. "*Are you lost?*"

"*Hi,*" the dog replied. "*Yes, I am. I just escaped from a lab—I was part of an experiment and didn't want to be in it anymore. I just want to run free. I don't want to hurt anyone.*"

"It's okay," Bubbles called out to her sisters. "He's just lost, like I said." Buttercup and Blossom flew over.

"Wow, his fur is so soft," Blossom said, stroking the dog's head. The dog wagged its tail happily as Blossom continued to pet it.

"And his nose is cold," Buttercup giggled, rubbing it.

Bubbles hugged the giant dog. It certainly seemed friendly! But where did it come from? What was this mysterious experiment? And who was responsible?

If Bubbles asks the dog to show them where he escaped from, turn to page 35.

If Bubbles asks the dog more questions about the lab experiment, turn to page 24.

Bubbles decided that she was better off agreeing with at least *one* of her sisters, and she really didn't want to attack the dog until she was sure it was dangerous.

"We'll watch the dog, as Blossom suggested," Bubbles announced.

Suddenly, the dog began growling. Then the dog opened its mouth wide—and jets of flame shot out!

"I've never seen a dog do *that!*" Buttercup cried, and her sisters nodded. Now the dog was *definitely* dangerous!

"I've got a plan," Blossom announced, then told her sisters about it. For once, Buttercup didn't argue. Then the Girls leaped into action!

Buttercup used her super-strength to stop the dog from stepping on people and cars. Blossom used her ice breath to put out the dog's fire. Then Bubbles approached the dog.

"*Please don't wreck Townsville anymore,*" she said to the dog.

"*Oh, I won't,*" it replied. "*I don't know what got into me—suddenly I felt angry and started breathing fire.*"

"*Where did you come from?*" Bubbles asked it.

"*Some monkey with a big helmet stuck me in a lab,*" the dog told her.

*It had to have been Mojo Jojo!* thought Bubbles.

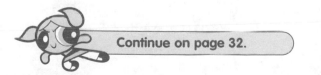

Continue on page 32.

"*He fed me chemicals that made me grow to this size,*" the dog continued. "*Today, I broke out of my cage and escaped. I didn't mean to cause any trouble.*"

Bubbles told her sisters what the dog had said. Blossom moved closer to the dog and noticed that its collar was strange—it looked like some kind of machine.

Blossom grabbed the collar and snapped it in half.

"*Thanks,*" the dog said. "*I was starting to get warm again and to feel angry for no reason.*"

"The collar was making the dog attack," Blossom decided.

"*I don't want to hurt anyone,*" the dog told Bubbles. "*I just want to go live peacefully in the woods.*"

"*Go on,*" Bubbles told him. "*No one will bother you anymore.*"

After the dog said good-bye and walked away, the Girls zoomed off to Mojo Jojo's lair. The sinister monkey mastermind was working on some nasty-looking machine when the Girls picked him up and dumped him in his usual jail cell.

"You know," Bubbles commented as the Girls were heading home, "when the dog started breathing fire, you two forgot you were arguing with each other and worked together again."

"You're right," Blossom said. "I guess we didn't really have anything important to fight about."

Buttercup nodded. "I guess not." She smiled. "Friends?"

Blossom smiled, too. "Friends."

Continue on page 64.

**33**

As Bubbles approached the dog, she saw that it had started to scratch at its collar. The next thing she knew, the dog was growling and barking, its fur bristling. Then the dog started breathing fire!

*Okay*, Bubbles thought, backing away, *maybe it isn't peaceful, after all!* She considered going after the dog on her own, but realized that it seemed too big and strong for her to handle alone. She needed her sisters, after all!

She flew back to the classroom and was amazed to find Buttercup and Blossom still squabbling over the blue crayon!

"Forget about the dumb crayon," Bubbles told them. "There's an enormous dog outside the classroom, and it's breathing fire! We need to stop it before it hurts anyone!"

Her sisters dropped the crayon at Bubbles's words.

"You're right; that *is* a problem," Blossom admitted.

"Yeah, let's get him!" Buttercup agreed. "Sorry, Ms. Keane, but we need to go save the day!"

Ms. Keane waved, and the three Girls flew outside after the giant dog.

Continue on page 55.

"*Could you show us where you escaped from?*" Bubbles asked the dog.

"*Sure,*" the dog replied.

"Come on, Girls!" called Bubbles to her sisters. "We're going to find that nasty secret lab."

The Girls followed the dog to the very center of Townsville Park—to the lair of the sinister monkey mastermind, Mojo Jojo!

"*I jumped down from there,*" the dog told Bubbles, gesturing up at Mojo's Volcano Top Observatory. "*Good thing I'm so big!*"

"Well, we'd better deal with Mojo," Blossom said. "Come on, Girls." She flew up to Mojo's hideout, with Buttercup right behind her, followed by Bubbles, who carried the dog with her.

The Girls and dog floated through the lair quietly, but Mojo didn't seem to be home.

"Ah, we should just go find him and dump him in jail," Buttercup said finally.

"No, we should take advantage of Mojo's absence to look around," Blossom argued. "We might find something to tell us more about how he's controlling this poor dog."

Bubbles sighed. Her sisters couldn't agree—again. Bubbles would have to decide what to do!

If Bubbles thinks the Girls should go looking for Mojo, as Buttercup suggested, turn to page 58.

If Bubbles thinks the Girls should look around Mojo's lair for clues, as Blossom suggested, turn to page 36.

"I think we should look around Mojo's lair for clues first," Bubbles decided. Blossom smiled at that, but Buttercup scowled.

"Then we can find Mojo," Bubbles quickly added. That made Buttercup brighten up, too.

The Girls spread out and searched Mojo's lab. There were many strange devices, but nothing seemed to relate to the dog's situation, until Buttercup stumbled onto a gadget labeled ANIMAL CONTROL BROADCAST UNIT.

"Hey, I think I found it!" Buttercup announced, and Bubbles and Blossom quickly flew to join her.

"Yes, that's it all right," Blossom agreed. "We should destroy it now, while we can."

Blossom focused her eye beams on the broadcast unit, but Mojo had built it well, and it withstood the attack. Blossom tried her eye beams again, but the unit still resisted. Then Bubbles added her eye beams, and the unit seemed to shake slightly. Then Buttercup added hers, and the unit crumbled into dust.

"Yay!" Buttercup cheered.

"Where's the dog?" Bubbles asked. They looked around quickly, and finally found him curled up in a corner, napping.

"*Sorry,*" the dog told Bubbles when she woke it up. "*I was starting to feel all angry, and my collar hurt, then it stopped and I felt fine. So I took a nap.*"

"The device was making the dog angry," Blossom realized. "It must have been broadcasting to the dog's collar."

The Girls destroyed the collar—which actually looked more like a tiny machine—just to be safe.

"*Thanks,*" the dog said. "*That's much better. Can I go now? I won't cause any trouble—I thought I'd go live in the woods, where I won't bother anyone—or be bothered.*"

The Girls agreed to let it go and waved good-bye as the dog left.

"None of us could have handled that gadget alone," Bubbles pointed out afterward. "It took all three of us together. Without fighting."

Blossom and Buttercup looked at each other.

"You're right—we were being stubborn, weren't we?" Blossom admitted. "I'm sorry."

"Me, too," Buttercup replied. "Now let's all go get Mojo together!"

The three Girls flew off together and finally located Mojo in a pet store, buying more animals for his experiments! Well, not anymore! The Girls put Mojo in jail and headed home.

Continue on page 64.

"Looks okay from here," Buttercup commented as the Girls neared the park.

"What's going on over there?" Blossom asked. The other Girls followed the direction of Blossom's gaze and saw that Townsville's water tower, which stood at the far end of the park, seemed to be swaying.

The Powerpuff Girls zipped over to take a look, and, as they got closer, they spotted The Gangreen Gang! The Gang had two ropes tied to the tower, one on either side, and they were tugging on the ropes.

"Hey!" Blossom shouted. "They're using the tower for a tug-of-war!" She was right—and the tower was starting to look pretty wobbly!

"Let's get 'em!" Buttercup insisted.

"No, wait," said Blossom. "We should grab the tower instead, to keep it from falling over."

The two started arguing about which plan they should use, and finally both of them looked at Bubbles.

If Bubbles suggests that the Girls follow Buttercup's plan to go after the Gangreen Gang, turn to page 40.

If Bubbles suggests that the Girls follow Blossom's plan to grab the water tower, turn to page 41.

"Please don't race!" Bubbles pleaded to her sisters, but Buttercup just laughed at her.

"What's the matter, not fast enough?" Buttercup said.

"We need to find Mojo!" Bubbles reminded her sisters.

"We'll find him—just as soon as I prove *I'm* faster," Blossom replied. Then the two of them sped off, leaving Bubbles behind.

Bubbles sighed. *Someone* had to look for Mojo— and, obviously, that someone would have to be Bubbles. She flew around Townsville, keeping an eye out for the evil monkey. Finally, Bubbles spotted him out in front of the bank. He was standing in the midst of a cloud of greenish gas, and a large radio was on the ground next to him. People were walking up to Mojo and offering him money and valuables, which he was putting in several large bags beside him. Mojo was so busy with the money that he hadn't noticed Bubbles yet. This was her chance! But maybe she should wait for her sisters.

If Bubbles goes after Mojo alone, turn to page 20.

If Bubbles waits for her sisters, turn to page 21.

Bubbles decided to side with Buttercup—it was better to grab the Gang before they could cause any more trouble.

"Let's just get the Gangreen Gang before they can topple the tower!" Bubbles said firmly.

Buttercup grinned. "Yeah!"

Blossom shook her head, but said, "Fine. Let's go, then."

Buttercup pulled Little Arturo away from the rope. But Ace and Snake still had hold of the rope. Blossom pushed Grubber away from his rope—but Big Billy was still there, and still pulling. Bubbles shoved Ace and Snake away, and Buttercup tossed Little Arturo aside again, but that left Big Billy without opposition, and he gave a powerful tug on his rope, almost pulling one of the tower's legs from the ground.

"This isn't going to work!" Blossom shouted finally. "Every time we get one of them away, one of the others grabs the rope!"

"I know, I know!" Bubbles shouted. "Go for the ropes instead!"

"I still think at least one of us should steady the tower," insisted Blossom.

If Bubbles and her sisters all go for the ropes, turn to page 43.

If Bubbles goes for the tower and leaves the ropes to her sisters, turn to page 44.

"I think we should follow Blossom's plan," Bubbles finally decided. "Saving the tower is more important, and if we hold it steady, the Gang can't pull it over."

"Fine, then," Buttercup grumbled. "Let's go." The Girls flew in over the Gangreen Gang and grabbed the water tower on three sides, holding it tight. The Gang wasn't able to budge it anymore. But that didn't seem to stop them.

"Cool, more of a challenge!" Ace shouted. "Okay, guys, let's give these Girls something to do!" And they started tugging twice as hard.

Then Bubbles had an idea.

"One of us should hold the tower," she told her sisters, "while the other two grab the ropes from the Gang members. That way we'll keep the tower steady, and stop them from pulling anymore."

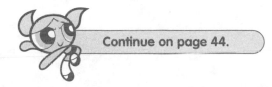

Continue on page 44.

"Blossom," Bubbles called out, "use your ice breath to stop the fire." Blossom nodded, and blew out a gust of freezing air, which put out the animals' flames.

"Buttercup, hold the animals back," Bubbles said next. Buttercup nodded and kept the oversized animals from getting any closer. Then Bubbles flew over to Mojo and grabbed him, while Blossom snatched the device from his hand. Blossom smashed it, and the animals calmed down instantly.

"*Sorry about that,*" the animals told Bubbles. "*That thing kept sending signals to our collars. Then the collars made us angry and caused the flames. We don't really want to hurt anyone.*"

The Girls destroyed the animals' collars, which were made of metal and studded with machine parts, then let the animals go.

"*We're going to live in the woods, where we won't hurt anyone—or be hurt by anyone,*" they told Bubbles as they left. "*Thanks again!*"

Then the Girls took Mojo to jail.

"It took all three of us to stop him, didn't it?" Buttercup admitted as they were flying home.

"Yes, it did," Blossom agreed. "And it took Bubbles to make us realize it. Good job, Bubbles."

"Yeah, nice work," Buttercup chimed in.

Continue on page 64.

42

"If we all go for the ropes, that should steady the tower," Bubbles said.

So Buttercup took the rope on the left, and Blossom grabbed the one on the right, shoving aside the Gangreen Gang members who still had hold of the ropes. Bubbles grabbed the same rope as Blossom.

"You're siding with Blossom—that's two against one!" Buttercup shouted. "But I'm still stronger!" And she started tugging on her rope.

"Oh, yeah?" Blossom shouted back, and tugged on her rope as well. Now it was The Powerpuff Girls, not the Gangreen Gang, having a tug-of-war!

"Stop!" cried Bubbles, letting go of her rope. Thankfully, both her sisters stopped their tugging.

"Your tug-of-war could have knocked over the water tower and flooded Townsville," Bubbles said sternly.

"Wow! You're right," Blossom admitted. "I guess we weren't thinking. I'm sorry."

"Yeah. Me, too," said Buttercup.

"We should be fighting people who deserve it—like the Gangreen Gang—not one another!" said Bubbles.

"Yeah!" chorused her sisters. The Powerpuff Girls made sure that the water tower was steady. Then the Girls again went after the Gangreen Gang, who had started running away when the Girls were tugging at the ropes. The Girls caught them all, and put the Gang in jail.

Continue on page 64.

Bubbles grabbed the water tower, steadying it, while Buttercup and Blossom each went for a rope. The Gang was knocked aside and ran off, but then Buttercup grinned at Blossom.

"Bet I'm stronger!" Buttercup taunted.

"You are *not!*" Blossom replied, and they both started tugging on their ropes.

"Stop that!" Bubbles shouted at them. "You're worse than the Gangreen Gang!" That made her sisters pause, and then they realized what they'd almost done. They could have flooded Townsville, all over a silly argument!

"I'm sorry," Buttercup said. "I just got carried away."

"Me, too," said Blossom. "I don't know why I got so mad at you, Buttercup."

"Just remember," Bubbles said, "it took all three of us to save the tower." Her sisters nodded, realizing Bubbles was right.

"And it'll take all three Powerpuff Girls to capture the Gangreen Gang!" added Buttercup.

"Let's go!" shouted Blossom.

And The Powerpuff Girls, together again, went off to find the Gangreen Gang and toss them in jail.

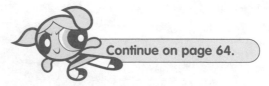

Continue on page 64.

"*I'm sorry,*" the dog said to Bubbles. "*The collar was making me attack and caused the flames.*"

Bubbles told her sisters what the dog had said, and they agreed that only one evil genius could have made a dog get so large and have created such a fiendish collar—Mojo Jojo! The Girls zoomed over to Mojo's hideout. The evil monkey was lounging around his lair, listening to classical music, and occasionally tinkering with a device labeled MACHINE TO CONTROL FIRE-BREATHING DOG COLLARS. Mojo barely had time to shout, "Girls? What are you doing here?" before Blossom, Buttercup, and Bubbles grabbed him and took him to jail.

The dog was allowed to go free. "*I'll go live in the woods, where I won't bother anyone—and won't be bothered by anyone,*" it told them.

Afterward, Blossom and Buttercup were both quiet. Bubbles guessed what they were thinking. "We're sisters," Bubbles said, "and a team. That's more important than who gets which crayon, or anything else that silly."

"You're right," Blossom admitted. "I *was* being silly. I'm sorry."

"I'm sorry, too," said Buttercup. "I'll save my fighting for the bad guys from now on."

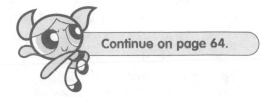

Continue on page 64.

Now that all three Girls were brainwashed, they didn't want to go after Mojo anymore—they *liked* him too much!

"Wow, Mojo's really cool," Buttercup said to her sisters.

"I know," Blossom agreed. "If only we had some money to give him!"

"We don't, though," Bubbles pointed out. "And we can't steal any—that wouldn't be right." Apparently, the Girls' sense of right and wrong was stronger than Mojo's brainwashing gas, which was lucky for Townsville!

The Girls watched Mojo taking people's money and putting it in bags, admiring how efficient he was. Next to Mojo was a radio, which was saying things like, "Mojo is your best friend. He is the greatest of monkey super-geniuses. Please give your best friend Mojo Jojo all of the money you have. And when you run out of your own money, steal some for Mojo." After a few minutes, though, Bubbles was struck by something.

"This is wrong, isn't it?" Bubbles asked her sisters. "I thought we *didn't* like Mojo. And why are people giving him their money?"

"Because they like him, silly," Buttercup replied. "He's our best friend, too." But she looked a little puzzled.

Suddenly, Bubbles understood. "It's the gas cloud!" she cried. "The cloud *made* us like him!"

"That's right," Blossom replied slowly. "It's making us *want* to give him money. But I think it's wearing off."

"And I was hit by it first," Bubbles agreed, "so I'm recovering first."

In less than a minute, all three Girls had shaken off the effects of Mojo's gas cloud.

"It must be our superpowers that let us get free of the cloud," Blossom decided. "None of the other people here at the bank seem to have recovered from it yet. But if we attack Mojo directly, he'll just hit us with more gas, and we'll like him all over again."

"Let's sneak up on him when he's not looking," Buttercup said, "and then we'll grab him!"

"But we need to go after the gas cloud and the radio, too, if we can," Blossom argued. "I think we should split up and each go after a separate target."

"Well," Buttercup replied, "since Bubbles got us into this mess, we'll let her decide!"

If Bubbles decides the Girls should sneak up on Mojo together, as Buttercup suggested, turn to page 56.

If Bubbles decides the Girls should split their efforts, as Blossom suggested, turn to page 52.

"I agree with Buttercup," Bubbles decided. "We should just go after Mojo!" Blossom shook her head in disagreement, but flew after her two sisters anyway.

All three of the Girls charged toward Mojo, but as they entered the gas cloud, they started to feel strange. They quickly landed in front of Mojo Jojo.

Bubbles remembered something about wanting to attack Mojo—but why would she want to do that? She *liked* Mojo—didn't she?

"Hello, Girls!" Mojo purred. "Would you like to give me, your best friend, some money?"

"We'd like to," Buttercup admitted. "But we don't have any."

"You could always steal some from somewhere— a jewelry store, perhaps," Mojo pointed out.

"No," Bubbles said, shaking her head. "That would be wrong. You're our friend—you wouldn't want us to do anything wrong." Apparently, the Girls' superpowered sense of right and wrong was more powerful than even Mojo's gas!

"Fine," Mojo finally said, frowning. "Have it your way!" And he walked away to take more money from some other brainwashed people.

The Girls watched him for a while.

"I like Mojo," Blossom finally said. "I *think*."

"I do, too," Buttercup agreed. "But that seems wrong."

"It *is* wrong!" Bubbles announced. "We *don't* like Mojo! It's the gas cloud! It was affecting us!" Her sisters shook their heads to clear them.

"It must be our superpowers that let us return to our senses," Blossom declared. "No one else here at the bank seems to have recovered yet."

"And if we go after him again, he'll just hit us with more of that stuff," Buttercup said. "We should all sneak up on him and grab him when he's not expecting it!"

"Or one of us could take care of him, while the other two go after the gas and that radio he's using," suggested Blossom.

"Well, I like *my* plan better," protested Buttercup.

"You *would*," said Blossom angrily.

Bubbles sighed. At least when the gas was affecting them, her sisters had agreed on *something*! Now they were back to arguing, and that meant she'd have to pick between their two plans!

If Bubbles decides that the Girls should sneak up on Mojo, as Buttercup suggested, turn to page 56.

If Bubbles decides that the Girls should split their efforts, as Blossom suggested, turn to page 52.

"Let's concentrate our eye beams all in one spot—that should be powerful enough to get rid of the gas!" Bubbles said. Blossom and Buttercup agreed and flew closer to Bubbles. The three Girls' combined eye beams hit the very same part of the cloud, burning it away completely. Then the Girls moved to another area of the cloud. The gas couldn't spread fast enough to get away from the Girls' eye beams. Soon the last of the gas was gone. Then Buttercup smashed the large radio next to Mojo; it had been broadcasting things like "Mojo is your best friend. Give Mojo all the money you can find."

"But, Girls," Mojo said, trying to smile. "You wouldn't want to do anything mean to me, your best friend, would you?"

"You were *never* our friend, Mojo Jojo,"

Buttercup told him, and the Girls flew Mojo off to jail, where he belonged.

Afterward, the Girls checked on the citizens of Townsville that Mojo had brainwashed. Without the gas cloud and the radio to reinforce Mojo's commands, the brainwashing wore off quickly.

"That was a good idea, Bubbles," Blossom commented. "Having us combine our eye beams really did the trick!"

"We always do work best together," Bubbles pointed out.

"You're right," Buttercup admitted. "I'm sorry about all the arguing, Blossom."

"Me, too," Blossom replied.

Continue on page 64.

51

"I think Blossom's plan is a good one," Bubbles said. "We need to take care of the *whole* problem—Mojo, the gas cloud, *and* the radio."

"Do I get to take care of Mojo?" Buttercup asked.

"Yes," Blossom replied. "*You* get to take care of him."

"Well, all right, then!" Buttercup cheered.

Blossom quickly outlined her plan, then the Girls launched into action!

Blossom attacked the gas cloud with her ice breath, freezing the cloud solid. Bubbles smashed the radio, which was saying "Mojo is your best friend" and "Give Mojo Jojo all your money." Buttercup grabbed Mojo, whose fur was thick with the now-frozen gas. Then all three Girls hauled Mojo to jail.

"Nice work, Girls," Blossom said.

"Well, it was a good plan," Buttercup admitted.

"And you two didn't fight about it," Bubbles pointed out.

"We never *should* fight each other," Buttercup said. "I'm sorry, Blossom."

"So am I," Blossom replied.

Continue on page 64.

"Mojo's my best friend," Bubbles told her sisters. "Why would I grab him? I just wish I had some money to give him. He's the greatest of all monkey super-geniuses, you know."

"That doesn't sound good," Buttercup muttered, and started towards Bubbles.

"Don't," Blossom warned. "It must be that gas cloud that's making Bubbles act so funny. If you go into it, you'll be affected, too."

"Well, what do we do, then?" Buttercup asked. Blossom whispered to her, and finally Buttercup nodded.

Suddenly, the two Girls made their move! Blossom turned her eye beams on the gas cloud, burning a path to Bubbles. Buttercup flew along that path of clean air, grabbed Bubbles, and pulled her clear!

Once she was out of the gas cloud, Bubbles shook off the effects quickly.

"Thanks! Now that I'm unbrainwashed, I know how awful that gas was!" Bubbles said.

"Well," Blossom said, "we've got to get rid of that gas cloud before we can go after Mojo himself."

Continue on page 22.

Somehow, Bubbles just couldn't tell her sisters that she liked Mojo now.

"I'm not feeling so well," she said instead. "I think I'm too weak to capture him myself."

"Hang on, we'll help you!" Buttercup shouted, flying in. Blossom was right behind her, and soon all three of them were inside the gas cloud and under its brainwashing influence.

Continue on page 46.

The Girls flew over Townsville, searching for signs of the giant dog, and they were shocked to find a portion of the city in flames! And in the midst of the commotion was the giant dog—

stepping on cars, smashing into buildings, and breathing flames!

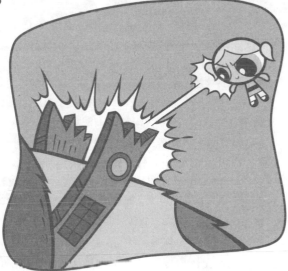

"After him, Girls!" called Blossom, and The Powerpuff Girls zoomed toward the dog. The Girls tried to climb on top of the dog to subdue it, but it shook them off like oversized fleas. Then Bubbles noticed the dog's collar. It was metal and studded with little pieces of machinery. Maybe the collar had something to do with the dog's destructive behavior! On a hunch, Bubbles used her eye beams to destroy the collar, and immediately the dog calmed down. Its flames also disappeared.

Continue on page 45.

"Let's sneak up on Mojo," whispered Bubbles to her sisters.

Mojo was too busy gathering up the money given to him by everyone else in the bank to pay attention to the Girls.

"Oh, no!" Mojo finally announced to the brainwashed crowd. "My money bags are full! I will need to go get new money bags since they have no more room in them. That way, all of you can continue to give me, your best friend, your money." With that, he hoisted the full bags on his shoulders and turned to walk back toward his lab.

"This is our chance," Blossom whispered, and her sisters nodded. The three of them floated a short distance behind Mojo so that he wouldn't see them. They waited until he was out of the gas cloud, then they leaped on Mojo.

"Gotcha, Mojo Jojo!" Buttercup shouted, landing on his shoulders and pinning him to the ground as his money bags went flying.

"Girls, is this any way to treat your best friend?" Mojo asked, assuming that the Girls were affected by the gas. The Girls just laughed at him.

"We don't make friends with criminals," Bubbles told him. They carried Mojo off to jail. Then they went back and turned off his radio and the gas canister. Without the gas and the radio's messages about giving Mojo money, everyone began to recover. And the police took charge of returning the money and valuables that Mojo had stolen from their rightful owners.

"I guess it *did* take all three of us to stop Mojo, didn't it?" Buttercup said later as they were heading home.

"Yes, it did, Buttercup," Blossom agreed. "And if you and I hadn't been fighting so much, we could have stopped him sooner."

"Well, you aren't fighting now," Bubbles pointed out. Her sisters both looked at each other and smiled, realizing she was right.

Continue on page 64.

"We need to find Mojo Jojo before he causes any more trouble," said Bubbles. Buttercup smiled at this, but Blossom looked upset. Finally, Blossom shrugged and followed her sisters as they zoomed out of the lab.

"*I can help you find the monkey,*" the dog told Bubbles. "*I've got a really good nose.*" The Girls agreed, and the dog led them through Townsville to a jewelry store. And there was Mojo, robbing the place!

"Now we've got you, Mojo!" Buttercup shouted as they burst inside the store, but Mojo didn't look at all worried. Instead, he pulled a small device from his belt and pressed a button.

"Ha-ha," Mojo cackled. "Now you will face the ferocity of my fierce animal friends, who are fierce and ferocious!"

Then the Girls heard a loud rumbling sound behind them. Glancing over their shoulders, they saw the dog, who was now growling at them!

"*I can't control it,*" the dog growled to Bubbles. "*I'm sorry!*" And then he began to breathe fire!

To make matters worse, the Girls heard other sounds as well, from outside the jewelry store— another heavy rumbling noise, plus a loud flapping noise. A moment later, the wall of the store crumbled, and in leaped a giant cat and a giant bird. And both of them were breathing fire as well!

Buttercup cried, "Let's get these oversized pets!"

"We shouldn't go after the animals," Blossom replied. "They probably wouldn't bother us if Mojo wasn't controlling them. We need to stop Mojo—and his device—first!"

Then both of them glanced at Bubbles—once again, she needed to pick which plan they'd use!

If Bubbles decides they should stop the animals first, as Buttercup suggested, turn to page 61.

If Bubbles decides they should go after Mojo and his device, as Blossom suggested, turn to page 14.

"The tornado, I think," said Bubbles. "Burning the gas with our eye beams might start a fire or something."

"I'll take care of this," said Buttercup. She started to whirl around in a circle, creating a tornado, which sucked up some of the gas cloud. But her tornado wasn't big enough to get all of the cloud. Bubbles joined her, and finally Blossom did as well. Now the tornado had all the gas trapped within it. Then the Girls sped outside of town, still spinning in circles to carry the tornado, and let the gas fade harmlessly into the sky. Townsville was saved! And minutes later, the Girls grabbed Mojo, who had been running from the bank, and put him back behind bars, where he belonged!

"Gee, I guess I couldn't do it myself, after all," Buttercup admitted afterward.

"No, but that was a good idea about the tornado," Blossom replied.

"It was," Bubbles commented, "but it took all three of us together to do it. That's because we work best together."

"You're right," Buttercup said. "I'm sorry I was fighting with you earlier, Blossom."

"Me, too," Blossom agreed.

Continue on page 64.

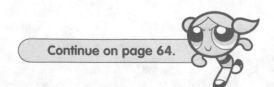

"I think we'd better stop the animals," Bubbles decided. "If we go after Mojo first, the animals could start causing more trouble."

The Girls leaped into action. But the giant, fire-breathing animals were very big and strong, and when the carpeting caught fire and began to smoke, it became difficult to see them. Once the smoke had cleared, the Girls realized they were alone in the store.

"Mojo—and the animals—got away!" Buttercup shouted.

"Well, we know where they're going," Blossom replied. "Mojo has to be going back to his lair. Let's go, Girls!"

The Girls quickly flew back to Mojo's hideout and crashed through the wall to find Mojo and the three large, fire-breathing animals.

"So," Mojo called out, "you come to meet your doom, here where your doom is, where you come to meet it! So be it!"

And the animals started to move toward The Powerpuff Girls. The Girls knew they couldn't fight the animals directly—the oversized pets were simply too strong. They needed something else.

If Bubbles suggests Blossom use her ice breath, turn to page 42.

If Bubbles looks around the lair for anything that might help them, turn to page 62.

*Mojo's lab is full of gadgets,* Bubbles thought, glancing around. *One of these weird devices must be able to help us with these animals.* Then she spied a large machine marked Animal Control Broadcast Unit. *That must be what's actually controlling the animals,* she realized. *Mojo's smaller device is just the remote control for this machine.*

"Buttercup, you hold back the animals," called Bubbles. "Blossom, you pin Mojo down. I'll destroy this machine—it's what's causing the animals to attack us!" Her sisters nodded, and did what Bubbles suggested.

Once Bubbles melted the broadcast unit with her eye beams, the animals' flames disappeared, and they grew calm. Then the Girls destroyed the animals' collars, which had been receiving the broadcast signals.

*"We're sorry,"* the animals told Bubbles. *"It was the collars that made us cause trouble. We'll go away now, into the woods, where we won't bother anyone—or be bothered by anyone."* The Girls let them go, and took Mojo to jail.

"That was a good plan, Bubbles," Blossom admitted.

"That's because we worked together," said Bubbles. "We're a team!"

"You're right, Bubbles," Buttercup said. "Blossom, I'm sorry I was arguing with you before."

"I'm sorry, too," said Blossom.

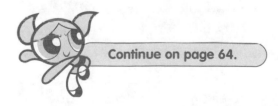

Continue on page 64.

Bubbles was very happy now that her sisters had apologized to each other and The Powerpuff Girls were a team again!

"We should say sorry to you, too, Bubbles, for sticking you in the middle while we were arguing," said Blossom.

"Blossom's right," said Buttercup. "You shouldn't have to fix things when Blossom and I fight."

"That's okay," Bubbles replied. "We're sisters. We help one another out."

When the Professor got home from his conference, he found the three Girls sitting on the sofa together, with Bubbles in the middle, giggling.

"And how was your day, Girls?" he asked.

"The *middle* was tough," Bubbles admitted, "but it ended well." And all of them laughed.

> *So once again, the day is saved, thanks to The Powerpuff Girls—especially Bubbles, who showed that being sweet doesn't mean you can't be strong!*

**THE END**